The Harry Potter Cocktail Cookbook

55 Amazing Drink Recipes for Wizards and Non-Wizards Alike

Jessica Woods

© Copyright 2020 – All rights reserved.

The content contained within this book may not be reproduced, duplicated or transmitted without direct written permission from the author or the publisher.

Under no circumstances will any blame or legal responsibility be held against the publisher, or author, for any damages, reparation, or monetary loss due to the information contained within this book, either directly or indirectly.

Legal Notice:

This book is copyright protected. It is only for personal use. You cannot amend, distribute, sell, use, quote or paraphrase any part, or the content within this book, without the consent of the author or publisher.

Disclaimer Notice:

Please note the information contained within this document is for educational and entertainment purposes only. All effort has been executed to present accurate, up to date, reliable, complete information. No warranties of any kind are declared or implied. Readers acknowledge that the author is not engaged in the rendering of legal, financial, medical or professional advice. The content within this book has been derived from various sources. Please consult a licensed professional before attempting any techniques outlined in this book.

By reading this document, the reader agrees that under no circumstances is the author responsible for any losses, direct or indirect, that are incurred as a result of the use of the information contained within this document, including, but not limited to, errors, omissions, or inaccuracies.

Table of Contents

Introduction 5

Butter Beer Cocktail 6

Draught of Living Death 7

Death Eater's Draught 8

Unicorn Blood Cocktail 9

Polyjuice Potion 10

Goblet of Fire 11

Phoenix Feather 12

Witches Brew Cocktail 13

Polyjuice Potion Jelly Shots 14

Pumpkintini 15

Three Broomstick's Gillywater 16

Rubeus Hagrid Cocktail 17

Hermione Granger Cocktail 18

Ronald Weasley Cocktail 19

Sirius Black Cocktail 20

Amortentia Potion Punch 21

Black Magic Cocktail 22

Lord Voldemort Cocktail 23

Horcrux Cocktail 24

Golden Snitch Cocktail 25

Unicorn Kisses 26

Butterscotch Martini 27

Witch's Heart 29

Draco Malfoy Cocktail 30

Patronus Punch 32

Moaning Myrtle Cocktail 33

Charmed Cherry Soda 34

Buttered Fire Whisky 35

Felix Felicis Cocktail 36

Wolfsbane Potion 37

Pumpkin Juice Cocktail 38

Fizzing Whizzbee Cocktail 39

Hufflepuff Horizon Cocktail 40

Slytherin Savage Cocktail 41

Gryffindor's Goblet of Fire 42

Hogwarts Elixir Cocktail 43

Dementor's Kiss Cocktail 44

Lord Soda Cocktail 45

Conclusion.. 46

Introduction

Are you a Potterhead who would love to enjoy Harry Potter Inspired cocktails this holiday? Then it's about time to ride on the Hogwarts express and travel into the world of magical flavors and pleasing treats. Harry Potter and the series by Ms. J.K Rowling has ever been an inspiration for millions of its readers out there. Besides the mesmerizing portrayal of many of the imaginative characters, the drinks inspired by this series also bind the attention of millions of its fans and makes a great serving for holiday celebrations. Whether we want to party on Halloween or celebrate birthdays, the Harry Potter cocktail is essential to keep up with the theme. This Harry Potter Cocktail Recipes Cookbook' is therefore designed to bring you the best of the Wizardly cocktail recipes inspired by the amazing characters from the series. From Butterbeer to poly juice shots, this book will reveal all the deepest secrets of making the firing glass of goblet of fire.

Harry Potter Novel is a series of an era filled with the fascination of its imaginative and super creative content. Since 1997, J.K Rowling has made a big wave with the first ever of this series: Harry Potter and the Philosopher's Stone. Everyone was fascinated with the characters and the magical world the writer has created in the novel. Once you read and watch the Harry Potter movie, you feel like floating in the magical world of Harry and his friends. The charms of the spells, the fantasy of magic, and the fight against the evil, all the turns of events are so captivating that they leave us spellbound for hours. Winter holidays are that time of the year, where you get to spend your valuable time with your friends and family and to celebrate the festivities, you need to have fun and exciting drinks to share. The Harry Potter-inspired cocktails do not only taste amazing, but they also tend to a nice appeal to your drinks table. There are several varieties to try, from red unicorn blood drink to green Polyjuice shots; you will love how these cocktails look when served with dry ice. It's about time to ready your martini glasses and glass goblets to make some inspiring and exciting harry potter drinks in no time.

Butter Beer Cocktail

Prep Time: 5 minutes.
Cook Time: 0 minute.
Serves: 1

Ingredients:

- 1-ounce vanilla vodka
- 1-ounce butterscotch schnapps
- ½ ounce dark beer
- 10 ounces Jones cream soda
- Whipped cream

Preparation:

1. Add vodka, butterscotch, dark beer, cream soda to a cocktail shaker.
2. Shake the cocktail shaker for 1 minute.
3. Add ice and the prepared cocktail to a glass.
4. Garnish with whipped cream.
5. Serve.

Serving Suggestion: Serve the cocktail with chocolate syrup on top.

Variation Tip: Add a drizzle of chocolate-infused vodka for a strong taste.

Nutritional Information Per Serving:
Calories 289 | Fat 5g |Sodium 532mg | Carbs 44g | Fiber 0.4g | Sugar 44g | Protein 0.3g

Draught of Living Death

Prep Time: 5 minutes.
Cook Time: 0 minute.
Serves: 4

Ingredients:

- 2 ounces cranberry juice
- 1-ounce blue Curaçao
- 1-ounce vodka
- 1-ounce rum
- 1-ounce gin
- 6 ounces tonic water, chilled
- 1 cup crushed ice

Preparation:

1. Add vodka, butterscotch, dark beer, cream soda to a cocktail shaker.
2. Shake the cocktail shaker for 1 minute.
3. Add ice and the prepared cocktail to a glass.
4. Garnish with whipped cream.
5. Serve.

Serving Suggestion: Serve the cocktail with dry ice on top.

Variation Tip: Add a drizzle of lemon juice for a refreshing taste.

Nutritional Information Per Serving:
Calories 210 | Fat 5g |Sodium 32mg | Carbs 23g | Fiber 0.4g | Sugar 14g | Protein 1.3g

Death Eater's Draught

Prep Time: 5 minutes.
Cook Time: 0 minute.
Serves: 4

Ingredients:

- 1-ounce vodka
- 1-ounce blue curacao
- 1/2 ounces Midori or melon liqueur
- 1 ounce sweet and sour mix
- 3 ounces pineapple juice
- 1 teaspoon silver cake shimmer

Preparation:

1. Add vodka, blue curacao, Midori, sweet and sour mix, and pineapple juice to a cocktail shaker.
2. Shake the cocktail shaker for 1 minute.
3. Add dry ice and the prepared cocktail to a glass.
4. Garnish with silver cake shimmer.
5. Serve.

Serving Suggestion: Serve the cocktail with fresh cherries on top.

Variation Tip: Add a drizzle of spice-infused vodka for a strong taste.

Nutritional Information Per Serving:
Calories 105 | Fat 25g | Sodium 532mg | Carbs 38 | Fiber 0.4g | Sugar 12g | Protein 1.1g

Unicorn Blood Cocktail

Prep Time: 5 minutes.
Cook Time: 0 minute.
Serves: 4

Ingredients:

Raspberry Puree

- 7 ounces raspberries
- Icing sugar, to taste
- 4 tablespoons water

Shimmery Liqueur

- A pinch of purple luster petal dust

Preparation:

1. Blend raspberries, icing sugar, and water to a blender until smooth
2. Add dry ice and the prepared cocktail to the glasses.
3. Garnish with a purple luster
4. Serve.

Serving Suggestion: Serve the cocktail with fresh cherries on top.

Variation Tip: Add a drizzle of lemon juice for a refreshing taste.

Nutritional Information Per Serving:
Calories 190 | Fat 18g |Sodium 150mg | Carbs 16g | Fiber 0.4g | Sugar 4g | Protein 7.2g

Polyjuice Potion

Prep Time: 5 minutes.
Cook Time: 0 minute.
Serves: 2

Ingredients:

- 1 cup of orange juice
- 3 tablespoons ginger tea
- 2 canned peaches, slices
- ½ cup sprite
- 1 drop green food coloring
- 4 tablespoons vodka

Preparation:

1. Add orange juice, ginger tea, peach slices, sprite, food coloring, and vodka to a blender.
2. Blend the mixture until smooth.
3. Serve.

Serving Suggestion: Serve the cocktail with orange zest on top.

Variation Tip: Add a drizzle of lemon juice for a refreshing taste.

Nutritional Information Per Serving:

Calories 267 | Fat 12g |Sodium 165mg | Carbs 39g | Fiber 1.4g | Sugar 22g | Protein 3.3g

Goblet of Fire

Prep Time: 5 minutes.
Cook Time: 0 minute.
Serves: 1

Ingredients:

- 1-ounce vodka
- 1-ounce blue curacao
- 3 ounces lemonade
- Pinch of cinnamon
- A splash of 151 proof rum

Preparation:

1. Add vodka, blue curacao, and lemonade to a cocktail shaker.
2. Shake the cocktail shaker for 1 minute.
3. Pour the cocktail into the serving glass.
4. Add a splash of 151 proof rum right before serving.
5. Light the drink on fire and drizzle cinnamon on top.
6. Serve.

Serving Suggestion: Serve the cocktail with a cinnamon stick in the glass.

Variation Tip: Add a drizzle of golden syrup for a sweet taste.

Nutritional Information Per Serving:

Calories 183 | Fat 15g |Sodium 402mg | Carbs 25g | Fiber 0.4g | Sugar 1.1g | Protein 10g

Phoenix Feather

Prep Time: 5 minutes.
Cook Time: 0 minute.
Serves: 1

Ingredients:

- 2 ounces of Lillet blanc
- 1 ½ ounce of Campari
- 1-ounce grapefruit juice
- 2 ounces club soda

Preparation:

1. Add Lillet blanc, Campari, grapefruit juice, and club soda to a cocktail shaker.
2. Shake the cocktail shaker for 1 minute.
3. Add ice and the prepared cocktail to the glass.
4. Serve.

Serving Suggestion: Serve the cocktail with lemon slices on top.

Variation Tip: Add a drizzle of lemon juice for a refreshing taste.

Nutritional Information Per Serving:

Calories 273 | Fat 22g |Sodium 517mg | Carbs 33g | Fiber 0.2g | Sugar 1.4g | Protein 16.1g

Witches Brew Cocktail

Prep Time: 5 minutes.
Cook Time: 0 minute.
Serves: 12

Ingredients:

- 6 cups orange juice
- 6 cups pomegranate juice
- 3 cups citrus vodka

Preparation:

1. Add orange juice, pomegranate juice, and citrus vodka to a cocktail shaker.
2. Shake the cocktail shaker for 1 minute.
3. Add ice and the prepared cocktail to the serving glasses.
4. Serve.

Serving Suggestion: Serve the cocktail with fresh cherries on top.

Variation Tip: Add a drizzle of lemon juice for a refreshing taste.

Nutritional Information Per Serving:

Calories 102 | Fat 7.6g |Sodium 545mg | Carbs 35g | Fiber 0.4g | Sugar 17g | Protein 7.1g

Polyjuice Potion Jelly Shots

Prep Time: 5 minutes.
Cook Time: 12 minutes.
Serves: 4

Ingredients:

Ginger Ale mixture

- 1/2 cup ginger ale
- 1 plain envelope gelatin
- 1/2 cup ginger vodka

Pineapple mixture

- 1/2 cup canned pineapple juice
- 1 envelope plain gelatin
- 1/2 cup pineapple vodka

Lime mixture

- 1/2 cup water
- 1 envelope plain gelatin

Preparation:

1. Add ginger ale and gelatin to a saucepan, mix and cook for 5 minutes on a simmer.
2. Remove this ginger ale pan from the heat and stir in ginger vodka.
3. Add pineapple juice and gelatin to a saucepan, mix and cook for 5 minutes on a simmer.
4. Remove this pan pineapple juice pan from the heat and stir in pineapple vodka.
5. Add water, and gelatin to a saucepan, mix and cook for 2 minutes on a simmer.
6. Remove it from the heat.
7. Divide the ginger ale mixture into the shot's glasses.
8. Then divide the pineapple mixture and then the lime mixture.
9. Allow the shots to cool and serve.

Serving Suggestion: Serve the cocktail shots with shredded coconuts on top.

Variation Tip: Add a crushed mint to the prepared potions before cooling them down.

Nutritional Information Per Serving:

Calories 282 | Fat 15g | Sodium 26mg | Carbs 20g | Fiber 0.6g | Sugar 13g | Protein 1g

Pumpkintini

Prep Time: 5 minutes.
Cook Time: 0 minute.
Serves: 2

Ingredients:

- 2 graham crackers sheets, crushed
- Ice, crushed
- 6 tablespoons white rum
- 6 tablespoons pureed pumpkin
- 1 1/2 tablespoon pure maple syrup
- 1/2 tablespoon whiskey
- 1 pinch of ground cinnamon
- 2 tablespoons coconut milk

Preparation:

1. Add white rum, pureed pumpkin, maple syrup, whiskey, cinnamon, and coconut milk to a cocktail shaker.
2. Shake the cocktail shaker for 1 minute.
3. Dip and coat the rim of the serving glasses with the crushed crackers.
4. Add ice and the prepared cocktail to the glasses.
5. Serve.

Serving Suggestion: Serve the cocktail with crushed nuts or pumpkin spice powder on top.

Variation Tip: Add a drizzle of brewed coffee for a strong taste.

Nutritional Information Per Serving:

Calories 237 | Fat 19g | Sodium 518mg | Carbs 27g | Fiber 1.5g | Sugar 14g | Protein 2g

Three Broomstick's Gillywater

Prep Time: 5 minutes.
Cook Time: 0 minute.
Serves: 2

Ingredients:

- 2 shots gin
- 2 shots of coconut water with pulp
- Fever tree tonic water
- 1 Cucumber, halved crosswise
- 2 mint leaves

Preparation:

1. Place the cucumber on the cutting surface and cut from the round side of each cucumber half into several slits.
2. Bend the cucumber and make a rim to fit the glass.
3. Place one ring in each serving glass.
4. Pour in gin, coconut water, tonic water, and mint leaves.
5. Serve.

Serving Suggestion: Serve the cocktail with basil leaves on top.

Variation Tip: Add a drizzle of lemon juice for a refreshing taste.

Nutritional Information Per Serving:
Calories 209 | Fat 7.5g | Sodium 321mg | Carbs 4.1g | Fiber 4g | Sugar 3.8g | Protein 4.3g

Rubeus Hagrid Cocktail

Prep Time: 5 minutes.
Cook Time: 0 minute.
Serves: 1

Ingredients:

- 1-ounce Kahlua
- 1-ounce vodka
- ½ glass Guinness
- 1 splash of coke

Preparation:

1. Add Kahlua, vodka, and Guinness to a cocktail shaker.
2. Shake the cocktail shaker for 1 minute.
3. Pour the prepared cocktail into a glass and garnish with a splash of coke.
4. Serve.

Serving Suggestion: Serve the cocktail with fresh cherries on top.

Variation Tip: Add a drizzle of spice-infused vodka for a strong taste.

Nutritional Information Per Serving:
Calories 199 | Fat 11.1g | Sodium 297mg | Carbs 24.9g | Fiber 1g | Sugar 2.5g | Protein 9.9g

Hermione Granger Cocktail

Prep Time: 5 minutes.
Cook Time: 0 minute.
Serves: 1

Ingredients:

- 1 ½ ounce gin
- ¾ ounces apricot brandy
- ¾ ounces sweet vermouth
- 1 teaspoon grenadine
- ¼ teaspoon lemon juice
- 1 tablespoon sugar
- 2 cherries

Preparation:

1. Add gin, apricot, sweet vermouth, grenadine, sugar, and lemon juice to a cocktail shaker.
2. Shake the cocktail shaker for 1 minute.
3. Pour the prepared cocktail into a glass and garnish with cherries.
4. Serve.

Serving Suggestion: Serve the cocktail with sliced lemons on top.

Variation Tip: Add a drizzle of apricot preserves for a refreshing taste.

Nutritional Information Per Serving:
Calories 100 | Fat 2g | Sodium 480mg | Carbs 24g | Fiber 2g | Sugar 10g | Protein 18g

Ronald Weasley Cocktail

Prep Time: 5 minutes.
Cook Time: 0 minute.
Serves: 2

Ingredients:

- 1 ½ ounce vodka
- ½ ounce peach schnapps
- 1 dash grenadine
- Lemonade, as much needed
- Half a peach, sliced
- Lemon slice
- Maraschino cherry

Preparation:

1. Add vodka, peach schnapps, and grenadine to a cocktail shaker.
2. Shake the cocktail shaker for 1 minute.
3. Pour the prepared cocktail into a glass and fill the glass with lemonade.
4. Garnish with peach slices, lemon slices, and cherry.
5. Serve.

Serving Suggestion: Serve the cocktail with crushed candies on top.

Variation Tip: Add a drizzle of spiced infused vodka for a strong taste.

Nutritional Information Per Serving:
Calories 180 | Fat 3.2g | Sodium 133mg | Carbs 32g | Fiber 1.1g | Sugar 1.8g | Protein 9g

Sirius Black Cocktail

Prep Time: 5 minutes.
Cook Time: 0 minute.
Serves: 1

Ingredients:

- 2 ounces bourbon
- ¾ ounces triple sec
- 1 tablespoon apricot brandy
- Juice of ½ lime
- Apricot skin

Preparation:

1. Add bourbon, triple sec, apricot brandy, and lime juice to a cocktail shaker.
2. Shake the cocktail shaker for 1 minute.
3. Pour prepared cocktail into the serving glass and garnish with apricot skin
4. Serve.

Serving Suggestion: Serve the cocktail with fig slices on top.

Variation Tip: Add a drizzle of fig juice for a refreshing taste.

Nutritional Information Per Serving:
Calories 229 | Fat 1.9 |Sodium 567mg | Carbs 19g | Fiber 0.4g | Sugar 16g | Protein 1.8g

Amortentia Potion Punch

Prep Time: 5 minutes.
Cook Time: 0 minute.
Serves: 10

Ingredients:

- 1-pint fresh red raspberries
- 1 cup fresh pomegranate seeds
- 4 cups water, boiled and cooled
- Ice cubes

Punch:

- 1 (750-ml) bottle Aperol
- 4 cups pomegranate juice
- 2 cups gin
- 2 (750-ml) bottles chilled rosé sparkling wine

Preparation:

1. Add water, pomegranate seeds, and raspberries to a Bundt pan.
2. Cover and place this pan in the freezer overnight.
3. Next day, blend Aperol, pomegranate juice, gin, and sparkling wine in a punch bowl.
4. Add the frozen raspberry ice ring on top.
5. Serve.

Serving Suggestion: Serve the cocktail with fresh cherries on top.

Variation Tip: Add a drizzle of lemon juice for a refreshing taste.

Nutritional Information Per Serving:
Calories 185 | Fat 11g | Sodium 355mg | Carbs 21g | Fiber 5.8g | Sugar 13g | Protein 4.7g

Black Magic Cocktail

Prep Time: 5 minutes.
Cook Time: 0 minute.
Serves: 1

Ingredients:

- 2 ½ ounce black vodka
- 3/4-ounce lime juice
- 3/4-ounce simple syrup
- ice

Preparation:

1. Add black vodka, lime juice, and simple syrup to a cocktail shaker.
2. Shake the cocktail shaker for 1 minute.
3. Divide in the martini glasses and add ice cubes.
4. Serve.

Serving Suggestion: Serve the cocktail with blackberries on top.

Variation Tip: Add a drizzle of blackberry juice for a refreshing taste.

Nutritional Information Per Serving:
Calories 122 | Fat 1.8g |Sodium 794mg | Carbs 25g | Fiber 8.9g | Sugar 16g | Protein 1.9g

Lord Voldemort Cocktail

Prep Time: 5 minutes.
Cook Time: 0 minute.
Serves: 1

Ingredients:

- 1-ounce tequila
- 1/3 ounces Tabasco sauce
- 1 jalapeno pepper

Preparation:

1. Blend tabasco sauce and jalapeno pepper in a small blender.
2. Squeeze the liquid out of this paste into a shot glass.
3. Pour tequila into the glass.
4. Garnish with jalapeno and crushed ice.
5. Serve.

Serving Suggestion: Serve the cocktail with basil leaves on top.

Variation Tip: Add a drizzle of lemon juice for a refreshing taste.

Nutritional Information Per Serving:
Calories 163 | Fat 11.5g | Sodium 918mg | Carbs 8.3g | Fiber 4.2g | Sugar 0.2g | Protein 7.4g

Horcrux Cocktail

Prep Time: 5 minutes.
Cook Time: 0 minute.
Serves: 2

Ingredients:

- ¾ ounces tequila
- ¾ ounces vodka
- ¾ ounces triple Sec
- ¾ ounces gin
- ¾ ounces light rum
- 1-ounce sour Mix
- 1 splash coke
- Licorice stick, to garnish

Preparation:

1. Add tequila, vodka, triple sec, gin, light rum, and sour mix to a cocktail shaker.
2. Shake the cocktail shaker for 1 minute.
3. Divide into the glasses and garnish with coke and licorice.
4. Serve.

Serving Suggestion: Serve the cocktail with fresh cherries on top.

Variation Tip: Add a drizzle of sugar syrup for a refreshing taste.

Nutritional Information Per Serving:
Calories 134 | Fat 5.9g | Sodium 343mg | Carbs 29.5g | Fiber 0.5g | Sugar 11g | Protein 1.4g

Golden Snitch Cocktail

Prep Time: 5 minutes.
Cook Time: 0 minute.
Serves: `1

Ingredients:

- 1-ounce bailey's Irish cream
- 1-ounce gold schlager

Preparation:

1. Add bailey's Irish cream and gold schlager to a cocktail shaker.
2. Shake the cocktail shaker for 1 minute.
3. Serve.

Serving Suggestion: Serve the cocktail with orange slices on top.

Variation Tip: Add a drizzle of ginger ale for a refreshing taste.

Nutritional Information Per Serving:
Calories 186 | Fat 3g |Sodium 223mg | Carbs 31g | Fiber 8.7g | Sugar 5.5g | Protein 9.7g

Unicorn Kisses

Prep Time: 5 minutes.
Cook Time: 0 minute.
Serves: 1

Ingredients:

- 5 ounces strawberry lemonade
- 1 ounce blue raspberry vodka
- ½ ounce grenadine
- ¼ teaspoon lilac pearl dust
- Silver star glitter garnish
- Ice, crushed

Preparation:

1. Add strawberry lemonade, vodka, grenadine, and pearl dust to a cocktail shaker.
2. Shake the cocktail shaker for 1 minute.
3. Pour the prepared cocktail into a glass and garnish with start glitter and ice.
4. Serve.

Serving Suggestion: Serve the cocktail with lavender flowers on top.

Variation Tip: Add a drizzle of orange juice for a refreshing taste.

Nutritional Information Per Serving:
Calories 103 | Fat 8.4g |Sodium 117mg | Carbs 35g | Fiber 0.9g | Sugar 15g | Protein 5.1g

Butterscotch Martini

Prep Time: 5 minutes.
Cook Time: 0 minute.
Serves: 2

Ingredients:

- 1 ½ ounce vanilla vodka regular
- 1-1/2 ounces butterscotch schnapps
- 4 ounces cream soda
- 2 ounces Sprite

Preparation:

1. Add vodka, butterscotch schnapps, cream coda, and sprite to a cocktail shaker.
2. Shake the cocktail shaker for 1 minute.
3. Serve.

Serving Suggestion: Serve the cocktail with sliced olives on top.

Variation Tip: Add a drizzle of gin for a refreshing taste.

Nutritional Information Per Serving:

Calories 107 | Fat 8.6g |Sodium 510mg | Carbs 22.2g | Fiber 1.4g | Sugar 13g | Protein 3.6g

Flaming Dragon's Blood Cocktail

Prep Time: 5 minutes.
Cook Time: 0 minute.
Serves: 1

Ingredients:

- 1 ¾ jigger of Bacardi Superior rum
- 1 jigger thyme and raspberry syrup
- ½ jigger lemon juice
- 2 ice cubes, crushed
- ⅛ teaspoon of white luster dust
- 2 teaspoons Bacardi rum 151

Preparation:

1. Add Bacardi, raspberry syrup, lemon juice, ice cubes, and luster dust to a cocktail shaker.
2. Shake the cocktail shaker for 1 minute.
3. Pour the cocktail into the serving glass.
4. Add a splash of 151 Bacardi rum right before serving.
5. Light the drink on fire.
6. Serve.

Serving Suggestion: Serve the cocktail with raspberries on top.

Variation Tip: Add a drizzle of orange juice for a refreshing taste.

Nutritional Information Per Serving:
Calories 284 | Fat 7.9g | Sodium 704mg | Carbs 38.1g | Fiber 1.9g | Sugar 19g | Protein 4.8g

Witch's Heart

Prep Time: 5 minutes.
Cook Time: 0 minute.
Serves: 4

Ingredients:

- 1 jigger apple brandy
- 1 teaspoon grenadine
- 2 jiggers' blackberry shimmery liqueur
- Powdered dry ice
- Martini glass to serve

Preparation:

1. Add apple brandy and shimmery liqueur to a cocktail shaker.
2. Shake the cocktail shaker for 1 minute.
3. Fill the serving glass with 1 teaspoon of dry ice.
4. Pour the cocktail mixture into the glass.
5. Drizzle the grenadine on top.
6. Serve.

Serving Suggestion: Serve the cocktail with fresh cherries on top.

Variation Tip: Add a drizzle of strawberry juice for a refreshing taste.

Nutritional Information Per Serving:
Calories 113 | Fat 3g |Sodium 152mg | Carbs 20g | Fiber 3g | Sugar 11g | Protein 3.5g

Draco Malfoy Cocktail

Prep Time: 5 minutes.
Cook Time: 0 minute.
Serves: 2

Ingredients:

- 2 ounces gin
- 1 tablespoon dry vermouth
- 2 tablespoons olive juice
- 2 gruyere stuffed olives

Preparation:

1. Add gin, vermouth, and olive juice to a cocktail shaker.
2. Shake the cocktail shaker for 1 minute.
3. Pour the prepared cocktail into a glass filled with ice and garnish with olives.
4. Serve.

Serving Suggestion: Serve the cocktail with fresh cherries on top.

Variation Tip: Add a drizzle of lemon juice for a refreshing taste.

Nutritional Information Per Serving:

Calories 106 | Fat 3.4g |Sodium 174mg | Carbs 15g | Fiber 9.4g | Sugar 9g | Protein 1.6g

Fizzing Whizbees Levitator

Prep Time: 5 minutes.
Cook Time: 0 minute.
Serves: 2

Ingredients:

- 1 ½ ounce bourbon
- 1 ½ ounce simple syrup
- 1-ounce Campari
- ½ ounce lemon juice
- 1 egg white
- 3 ounces ginger ale
- 1 candy, crushed
- 1 Pop Rocks candy, crushed

Preparation:

1. Mix crushed candies in a plate and dip the rim of the serving glasses in the candies.
2. Add bourbon, simple syrup, Campari, lemon juice, egg white, and ginger ale to a cocktail shaker.
3. Shake the cocktail shaker for 1 minute.
4. Divide in the prepared glasses
5. Serve.

Serving Suggestion: Serve the cocktail with fresh cherries on top.

Variation Tip: Add a drizzle of orange juice for a refreshing taste.

Nutritional Information Per Serving:

Calories 170 | Fat 14.6g |Sodium 394mg | Carbs 31.3g | Fiber 7.5g | Sugar 9.7g | Protein 6.4g

Patronus Punch

Prep Time: 5 minutes.
Cook Time: 0 minute.
Serves: 4

Ingredients:

- 1 can limeade concentrate
- 1-liter tonic water
- 2-liter lemon-lime soda
- Fresh mint
- 1½ cup vodka

Preparation:

1. Add limeade concentrate, tonic water, lemon-lime soda, and vodka to a cocktail shaker.
2. Shake the cocktail shaker for 1 minute.
3. Divide in the serving glasses and garnish with fresh mint.
4. Serve.

Serving Suggestion: Serve the cocktail with basil leaves on top.

Variation Tip: Add a drizzle of jalapeno juice for a spicy taste.

Nutritional Information Per Serving:
Calories 231 | Fat 9g |Sodium 271mg | Carbs 32.8g | Fiber 6.4g | Sugar 17g | Protein 6.3g

Moaning Myrtle Cocktail

Prep Time: 5 minutes.
Cook Time: 0 minute.
Serves: 2

Ingredients:

- 2 ounces Champagne
- 1-ounce vodka
- 2 ounces white grape juice
- Purple sugar, to taste
- Dry Ice

Preparation:

1. Add champagne, vodka, white grape juice, and purple sugar to a cocktail shaker.
2. Shake the cocktail shaker for 1 minute.
3. Divide in the serving glasses, filled with dry ice.
4. Serve.

Serving Suggestion: Serve the cocktail with lavender flowers on top.

Variation Tip: Add a drizzle of lemon juice for a refreshing taste.

Nutritional Information Per Serving:

Calories 250 | Fat 2.6g | Sodium 358mg | Carbs 34.6g | Fiber 14.4g | Sugar 13g | Protein 1.9g

Charmed Cherry Soda

Prep Time: 5 minutes.
Cook Time: 10 minutes.
Serves: 2

Ingredients:

- 2 cups black cherries
- 1/2 cup sugar
- 1/2 water
- 1 tablespoon lemon juice
- Setzer Soda Water
- 1 shot plain vodka
- 1 shot lemon-flavored vodka
- Ice

Preparation:

1. Add cherries, sugar, lemon juice, and water to a saucepan and cook for 10 minutes on a simmer with occasional stirring.
2. Mash the raspberries as you cook the cherries.
3. Strain the cherry mixture and pour it into a jar.
4. Refrigerate for at least 1 hour, then serve.

Serving Suggestion: Serve the cocktail with fresh cherries on top.

Variation Tip: Add a drizzle of lemon juice for a refreshing taste.

Nutritional Information Per Serving:
Calories 288 | Fat 6.9g |Sodium 761mg | Carbs 46g | Fiber 4g | Sugar 12g | Protein 9.6g

Buttered Fire Whisky

Prep Time: 5 minutes.
Cook Time: 0 minute.
Serves: 2

Ingredients:

- 4 ounces cinnamon whiskey
- 12 ounces butterscotch soda
- 1-ounce Bacardi rum

Preparation:

1. Add cinnamon whiskey, butterscotch soda, and Bacardi rum to a cocktail shaker.
2. Shake the cocktail shaker for 1 minute.
3. Serve.

Serving Suggestion: Serve the cocktail with long orange zest strips in the glass.

Variation Tip: Add a drizzle of lemon juice for a refreshing taste.

Nutritional Information Per Serving:
Calories 212 | Fat 11.8g |Sodium 321mg | Carbs 24.6g | Fiber 4.4g | Sugar 8g | Protein 7.3g

Felix Felicis Cocktail

Prep Time: 5 minutes.
Cook Time: 0 minute.
Serves: 2

Ingredients:

- ¼ ounces simple syrup
- ¼ ounces lemon juice
- 1 ½ ounce ginger beer
- Champagne

Preparation:

1. Add simple syrup, lemon juice, and ginger beer to a cocktail shaker.
2. Shake the cocktail shaker for 1 minute.
3. Divide into the serving glasses and fill the rest with champagne
4. Serve.

Serving Suggestion: Serve the cocktail with lemon slices on top.

Variation Tip: Add a drizzle of orange juice for a refreshing taste.

Nutritional Information Per Serving:

Calories 260 | Fat 16g |Sodium 585mg | Carbs 31g | Fiber 1.3g | Sugar 12g | Protein 2.5g

Wolfsbane Potion

Prep Time: 5 minutes.
Cook Time: 0 minute.
Serves: 1

Ingredients:

- 1 ½ ounce Scotch whiskey
- 1 ½ ounce Fernet-Branca
- Coca-Cola

Preparation:

1. Add scotch whiskey and fernet Branca to a cocktail shaker.
2. Shake the cocktail shaker for 1 minute.
3. Pour the prepared cocktail into the serving glass and fill the rest with coco cola
4. Serve.

Serving Suggestion: Serve the cocktail with fresh cherries on top.

Variation Tip: Add a drizzle of blue curacao for a refreshing taste.

Nutritional Information Per Serving:
Calories 266 | Fat 6.3g |Sodium 193mg | Carbs 39.1g | Fiber 7.2g | Sugar 15.2g | Protein 1.8g

Pumpkin Juice Cocktail

Prep Time: 5 minutes.
Cook Time: 15 minutes.
Serves: 6

Ingredients:

- 8 cups apple cider
- 1 (15 ounces) can pumpkin puree
- 2 cups apricot nectar
- 1/4 cup brown sugar
- 3/4 teaspoon ground cinnamon
- 1/4 teaspoon ground nutmeg
- 1/4 ground ginger
- 1 pinch of ground allspice
- 2 teaspoons vanilla

Preparation:

1. Add apple cider, pumpkin puree, apricot nectar, brown sugar, ground cinnamon, nutmeg, ginger, and allspice to a saucepan.
2. Cook this mixture on a simmer for 15 minutes.
3. Remove it from the heat and stir in vanilla, then allow it to cool.
4. Serve.

Serving Suggestion: Serve the cocktail with pumpkin spice on top.

Variation Tip: Add a drizzle of apple juice for a refreshing taste.

Nutritional Information Per Serving:
Calories 297 | Fat 1g |Sodium 291mg | Carbs 35g | Fiber 1g | Sugar 9g | Protein 2g

Fizzing Whizzbee Cocktail

Prep Time: 5 minutes.
Cook Time: 0 minute.
Serves: 2

Ingredients:

- 4 ounces tequila
- 16 ounces diet tonic
- Juice of ½ a lime
- Juice of ½ an orange
- Zest of ½ orange and
- Zest of 1/2 lime
- 1/4 cup sugar

Preparation:

1. Mix orange zest, lime zest, and sugar and coat the rim of the glasses with this mixture
2. Add tequila, tonic, lime juice, and orange juice to a cocktail shaker.
3. Shake the cocktail shaker for 1 minute.
4. Divide the cocktail into the prepared glasses.
5. Serve.

Serving Suggestion: Serve the cocktail with fresh thyme on top.

Variation Tip: Add a drizzle of grapefruit juice for a refreshing taste.

Nutritional Information Per Serving:
Calories 148 | Fat 30g |Sodium 660mg | Carbs 15g | Fiber 0g | Sugar 10g | Protein 1g

Hufflepuff Horizon Cocktail

Prep Time: 5 minutes.
Cook Time: 0 minute.
Serves: 4

Ingredients:

- 1.7 ounces passionfruit juice
- 1.7 ounces orange juice
- 2 ½ ounce tequila
- 4 fresh basil leaves
- 2 sprigs fresh mint
- 2 tablespoons white sugar
- 1 lime, cut in quarters
- Black salt, for the rim

Preparation:

1. Dip and coat the rim of the serving glasses with water and black salt.
2. Add juices, tequila, basil leaves, mint, and white sugar to a cocktail shaker.
3. Shake the cocktail shaker for 1 minute.
4. Divide into the serving glasses and garnish with lime quarters.
5. Serve.

Serving Suggestion: Serve the cocktail with fresh basil on top.

Variation Tip: Add a drizzle of lemon juice for a refreshing taste.

Nutritional Information Per Serving:
Calories 257 | Fat 10.4g |Sodium 431mg | Carbs 20g | Fiber 0g | Sugar 1.6g | Protein 1g

Slytherin Savage Cocktail

Prep Time: 5 minutes.
Cook Time: 0 minute.
Serves: 2

Ingredients:

- 1.7 ounces DE Kuyper Apple Schnapps
- 1.7 ounces jalapeño-infused vodka
- 2 /3 ounces simple syrup
- 2 drops Angostura bitters
- A drizzle of blackberry syrup
- Black salt, for the rim
- Blackberries and jalapeño slices for garnish

Preparation:

1. Dip and coat the rim of the serving glass with water and black salt.
2. Add apple schnapps, vodka, simple syrup, bitter, and blackberry syrup to a cocktail shaker.
3. Divide the cocktail into the serving glasses.
4. Garnish with blackberries and jalapeno.
5. Serve.

Serving Suggestion: Serve the cocktail with fresh basil leaves on top.

Variation Tip: Add a drizzle of lemon juice for a refreshing taste.

Nutritional Information Per Serving:
Calories 199 | Fat 16g |Sodium 537mg | Carbs 28g | Fiber 3g | Sugar 10g | Protein 3g

Gryffindor's Goblet of Fire

Prep Time: 5 minutes.
Cook Time: 0 minute.
Serves: 6

Ingredients:

Yellow Layer:

- 8 2/3 ounces frozen mango
- 1.7 ounces mango purée
- 1.7 ounces mango-flavored vodka
- 2/3 ounces peach Schnapps
- 1/2 teaspoon lime juice
- 2 drops citrus Angostura bitters

Red Layer:

- 8 2/3 ounces frozen strawberries
- 2 ½ ounce berry-flavored vodka
- 1.7 ounces Grenadine
- 1/2 teaspoon lime juice
- Tajin for the rim of the glass
- Candied chili mango, to garnish
- Peach gummy rings, to garnish

Preparation:

1. Dip and coat the rim of the serving glass with water and Tajin.
2. Blend strawberries, vodka, grenadine, and lime juice in a blender.
3. Divide this layer into the serving glasses.
4. Blend mango, puree, vodka, schnapps, lime juice, and butter in a blender.
5. Pour this mixture over the red layer.
6. Garnish with chili mango and gummy peach rings.
7. Serve.

Serving Suggestion: Serve the cocktail with raspberry syrup on top.

Variation Tip: Add a drizzle of pineapple juice for a refreshing taste.

Nutritional Information Per Serving:

Calories 205 | Fat 15g | Sodium 482mg | Carbs 27g | Fiber 3g | Sugar 2g | Protein 3g

Hogwarts Elixir Cocktail

Prep Time: 5 minutes.
Cook Time: 0 minute.
Serves: 2

Ingredients:

- 3 ounces double espresso vodka
- 1-ounce RumChata
- Whipped cream
- Chocolate shavings

Preparation:

1. Add espresso vodka and RumChata to a cocktail shaker.
2. Shake the cocktail shaker for 1 minute.
3. Divide into the serving glasses and garnish with whipped cream and chocolate shavings.
4. Serve.

Serving Suggestion: Serve the cocktail with colorful sprinkles on top.

Variation Tip: Add a drizzle of brewed coffee for good taste.

Nutritional Information Per Serving:
Calories 236 | Fat 6g | Sodium 181mg | Carbs 33g | Fiber 0.2g | Sugar 14g | Protein 1.2g

Dementor's Kiss Cocktail

Prep Time: 10 minutes.
Cook Time: 5 minutes.
Serves: 2

Ingredients:

Spiced syrup

- 3 cups of water
- 1 cinnamon stick
- 1 cardamom pod, cracked
- 1 pinch of nutmeg
- 1 teaspoon vanilla
- 1-star anise

Cocktail

- ½ cup Kahlua, coffee liqueur
- 1 cup Chocolate Vodka
- 1 cup spiced syrup

Preparation:

1. Add water, cinnamon stick, cardamom, nutmeg, vanilla, and star anise to a saucepan.
2. Cook the syrup for 5 minutes on a low simmer.
3. Strain the syrup and allow it to cool.
4. Add spiced syrup, Kahlua, and chocolate vodka to a cocktail shaker.
5. Shake the cocktail shaker for 1 minute.
6. Serve.

Serving Suggestion: Serve the cocktail with orange slices on top.

Variation Tip: Add a drizzle of orange juice for a refreshing taste.

Nutritional Information Per Serving:
Calories 143 | Fat 1g | Sodium 7mg | Carbs 40g | Fiber 1g | Sugar 39g | Protein 1g

Lord Soda Cocktail

Prep Time: 5 minutes.
Cook Time: 0 minute.
Serves: 2

Ingredients:

- 3 ounces of cranberry juice
- 2 ounces of soda
- Crushed ice

Preparation:

1. Add crushed ice with cranberry juice and soda in a cocktail shaker.
2. Shake the cocktail shaker for 1 minute.
3. Serve.

Serving Suggestion: Serve the cocktail with fresh cherries on top.

Variation Tip: Add a drizzle of lemon juice for a refreshing taste.

Nutritional Information Per Serving:
Calories 208 | Fat 24g | Sodium 715mg | Carbs 30.8g | Fiber 0.1g | Sugar 0.1g | Protein 1.9g

Conclusion

Did you like those harry potter cocktail recipes? Don't they take you back to a road trip to Hogwarts? Well, if you are reading this part of the book, then you must have already picked up your most favorite harry potter cocktail out of our collection. And if you are still wondering to select the best one out, then there is no better way than to try different cocktail recipes from this book and taste and test to find your drink.

In a nutshell, the content of this book brings you one step closer to the mystical world of wizardry in a way you might have never explored before. The intent behind creating these simple and amazing cocktail recipes was to bring magic into your home. Let your creativity shine in the kitchen and make the world taste the fineness of your cooking techniques. Do not forget to add something extra to style each cocktail in your own way. Be unique and amazing in your own ways.

There are a number of recipes that were either inspired by the Harry Potter series. Whether it was the use of some fine witchcraft or simple cooking techniques, these recipes wowed us with their irresistible appeal. On top of the list, some of these were:

- Butterbeer cocktail
- Pumpkintini cocktail
- Slytherin savage cocktail
- Hufflepuff Horizon cocktail

The entire length of this book discusses similar recipes and many others that are inspired by all the special moments of the series. From buttered fire whisky to golden snitch, each recipe is added, keeping in mind the beauty of Hogwarts. Now you don't need to be a Hogwarts graduate to be an expert to master the art of making magical cocktails; all it requires is to pick out your favorite recipe from this book and try it at home for you and your family.

CPSIA information can be obtained
at www.ICGtesting.com
Printed in the USA
LVHW061125231220
674972LV00003B/42